MW00877391

The ~~Twelve~~ 13 Dog Days of Christmas

A counting book for children.
By Melanie Johnston
Illustrated by Bob Reedy

ISBN 9781576382899
Library of Congress Control Number: 2015953276

This work was published in the United States of America by the

Merriam Press
133 Elm Street Suite 3R
Bennington VT 05201

merriam-press.com

This book belongs to:

_____

And was sniffed by:

_____

Dedicated to Floyde and Edy

On the first
my

A Pug

day of Christmas,
true love gave to me,

snoring
by a Pear Tree.

On the second day my

2 Basset

of Christmas,
true love gave to me,

Hounds,

 and a Pug snoring by a Pear Tree.

On the third
my true love gave

3 French

 2 Basset Hounds,

day of Christmas,
to me,

Bulldogs,

 and a Pug snoring by a Pear Tree.

On the fourth
my true love

4 Cocker

day of Christmas,
gave to me,

Spaniels,

and a Pug snoring by a Pear Tree.

On the fifth

5 Golden

 4 Cocker Spaniels, 3 French Bulldogs,

day of Christmas, my true love gave to me,

Retrievers...

 2 Basset Hounds, and a Pug snoring by a Pear Tree.

On the sixth day my true

6 Scotties

of Christmas,
love gave to me,

sniffing,

 2 Basset Hounds, and a Pug snoring by a Pear Tree.

On the seventh my true love gave

7 Setters

day of Christmas,
t me

swimming,

 3 French Bulldogs, 2 Basset Hounds,

 and a Pug snoring by a Pear Tree.

On the eighth
my

8 Labs

 7 Setters swimming, 6 Scotties sniffing, 5 Golden Retrievers

day of Christmas,
true love gave to me,

a leaping,

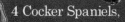4 Cocker Spaniels, 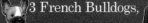3 French Bulldogs, 2 Basset Hounds,

and a Pug snoring by a Pear Tree.

On the ninth day
my true

9 Dalmations

of Christmas,
love gave to me,

dancing,

5 Golden Retrievers, 4 Cocker Spaniels, 3 French Bulldogs,

 2 Basset Hounds, 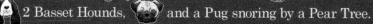 and a Pug snoring by a Pear Tree.

On the tenth day of my true

10 Dachshunds

 9 Dalmations dancing, 8 Labs a leaping, 7 Setters swimming,

3 French Bulldogs, 2 Basset Hounds,

Christmas,
love gave to me,

dashing,

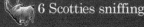 6 Scotties sniffing, 5 Golden Retrievers, 4 Cocker Spaniels,
 and a Pug snoring by a Pear Tree.

On the eleventh
my true

11 Boxers

day of Christmas,
love gave to me,

begging,

leaping, 7 Setters swimming, 6 Scotties sniffing,

 2 Basset Hounds, and a Pug snoring by a Pear Tree.

On the twelfth
my true

12 puppies

11 Boxers begging,   10 Dachshunds dashing,   9 Dalmations

5 Golden Retrievers,   4 Cocker Spaniels,   3 French Bulldogs,

day of Christmas,
love gave to me,

playing,

dancing, 8 Labs a leaping, 7 Setters swimming, 6 Scotties sniffing,

 2 Basset Hounds, and a Pug snoring by a Pear Tree.

On the thirteenth
day of Christmas,
my true love stopped
giving me dogs.

78 dogs
is a lotta dogs.

The End.

Part of the proceeds
from this book go to
Tony LaRussa's
Animal Rescue Foundation,
ARF.

Made in the USA
Columbia, SC
27 September 2019